A LITTLE SPOT OF CONFIDENCE

Written & Illustrated
by Diane Alber

To my children, Ryan and Anna:

When you believe in yourself, great things happen!

This book belongs to:

_____

_____

_____

Hi! I'm a CONFIDENCE SPOT!
I see you have some CONFIDENCE SPOTS already!

Your CONFIDENCE SPOT is there to help you
believe in yourself!

Your CONFIDENCE SPOT can usually be found on your shoulder or by your side. When it's on your shoulder, it's close to your ear so it can whisper words of encouragement. Its nickname can be "inner voice."

When your CONFIDENCE SPOT is by your side,
it will try and hold your hand to let you know
you're not alone. It will give you the strength to keep going.

Unlike some other SPOTS of emotion,
you want your CONFIDENCE SPOT TO GROW because it
helps you feel good about yourself.

Your ANXIETY SPOT and your CONFIDENCE SPOT are often
competing to see who's bigger. Because you don't feel good when
your ANXIETY SPOT is TOO BIG, your goal is to have your
CONFIDENCE SPOT WIN as the BIGGER SPOT!

But don't worry! I'm going to show you LOTS of ways your CONFIDENCE SPOT can GROW!

In fact, I'm going to tell you a secret...
Your family, teachers, and guardians were helping you grow
your CONFIDENCE SPOT even before you could remember.
When they were encouraging you to try new things and
teaching you how to believe in yourself, they were helping
you GROW your CONFIDENCE SPOT.

LOVE can help your
CONFIDENCE SPOT GROW.

Did you know YOU have the power to GROW your CONFIDENCE SPOT, too?

It's important that you learn how to recognize when you are feeling insecure or worried so you can focus on making yourself feel better.

KNOWLEDGE can help your
CONFIDENCE SPOT GROW.

Words are very powerful and can help you change the way you see yourself and how others see themselves, too.

If you don't feel like you can do something, repeating the words "I am brave" can help you do it!

AFFIRMATIONS can help your CONFIDENCE SPOT GROW.

Today is a new day! I will have a great start.
I will listen to the voice inside my heart.
I will let good thoughts inside my mind
and tell myself: I am brave, I am loving, I am kind.

Trying something new, gives you more opportunity to experience success!

CREATIVITY can help your CONFIDENCE SPOT GROW.

Setting small goals, like making your bed for a week, can help you accomplish more goals for yourself!

AMBITION can help your CONFIDENCE SPOT GROW.

Finding the energy to keep going even when you are tired can help you realize how strong you are.

ENDURANCE can help your CONFIDENCE SPOT GROW.

Sometimes it's scary to get up on stage or get
in front of a large group of people. But the more you do it,
the easier it becomes.

COURAGE can help your
CONFIDENCE SPOT GROW.

Doing nice things for others and saying nice things can GROW other people's CONFIDENCE SPOTS! And when you help others GROW their CONFIDENCE SPOT, YOURS GROWS, TOO!

KINDNESS can help your CONFIDENCE SPOT GROW!

I know sometimes it's hard to remember to be kind and that's why I'm here to help! All you need to do is place a SPOT on your hand, just like that!

Now, every time you SPOT me, do something

KIND!

Noticing all the wonderful things around you can help keep negative thoughts away that discourage you.

POSITIVITY can help your CONFIDENCE SPOT GROW!

When you make a mistake, instead of seeing it as a failure, see it as an opportunity to learn.

DETERMINATION can help your CONFIDENCE SPOT GROW!

When something seems impossible,
don't give up right away! Try again.

PERSISTENCE can help your
CONFIDENCE SPOT GROW!

Your body language says a lot about how you feel.
When you are standing up straight and looking
confident, it can actually make you feel better!

SMILING can help your CONFIDENCE SPOT GROW!

When you believe in yourself, great things happen!

Today is a new day! I will have a great start.
I will listen to the voice inside my heart.
I will let good thoughts inside my mind
and tell myself: I am brave, I am loving, I am kind.

Make copies of this affirmation card and place it where you will remember to grow your little SPOT of CONFIDENCE!

Made in the USA
Columbia, SC
31 July 2021